BALANCING THE BOOK

A SHORT STORY

ALEXANDRIA BLAELOCK

BlueMere Books
MELBOURNE, AUSTRALIA

For permission requests, please contact
enquiries@bluemerebooks.com.

Ordering Information:
Discounts are available on quantity purchases. For details, contact orders@bluemerebooks.com.

Balancing the Book/Alexandria Blaelock
paperback ISBN: 978-1-925749-30-4
digital ISBN: 978-1-925749-31-1

Book Layout © BookDesignTemplates.com

BlueMere Books
www.bluemerebooks.com

BALANCING THE BOOK

I was tired.

Wait.

Scrub that, I was exhausted.

It'd been a long tiring day at hospital, and I was way past ready to go home.

I wanted a long hot shower with a sandalwood body scrub to wash away the smell, and a long lie down.

And several large alcoholic beverages.

Not necessarily in that order.

I shouldn't complain.

I'm in remission, and the annual scans ensure I stay that way.

But, with all the requisite waiting, a ten-minute session in the machine ends up taking a day of your life.

And a month's worth of mobile data as you try to entertain yourself.

The least they could do to make it more bearable would be let you hook into their Wi-Fi network for free.

As if!

Howls of cynical laughter.

And all the while you're freezing your box off in a thin, backless paper robe, breathing dead oxygen-less air in a featureless institutional grey room that's super-cooled to keep the machinery operating at peak efficiency.

Your soul cries out for a spark of colour or light or warmth to break up the tedious dreariness of it all.

Like anything remotely interesting could kill you quicker than the cancer.

Or so it seems.

Not to mention the assumption that your white hair means you're a sweet, biddable old lady rather than an unhappy consequence of your treatment.

Actually, I don't really mind the deference that white hair brings me, but I do mind the relentless over-familiar cheerfulness, propensity to talk at you in baby talk and rubbing your half-naked back without asking.

And the offers of large print craft magazines instead of current affairs and political journals.

Urgh.

They really should know better.

But by the time your hospital visit is over, wilting in the full glare of the summer sun on a baking hot overground train station comes as a blessed relief.

Even though the languid breeze reeks of inadequate deodorant application, stale burgers and some kind of decomposing creature.

You can turn your face in any direction to see, smell and hear life happening all around you.

And even though you just want a bit of peace and quiet to let your soul unfurl, the overstuffed carriage of noisy hyperactive school children is generally a welcome change of pace.

Partly because they're bursting with life, but think they're dying because some boy/girl doesn't notice them, or Mum won't let them go to some concert/wear makeup/or hang out behind the basketball stadium with the other kids.

Naturally, I think we were better behaved at that age, but I find them more polite, respectful and amusing than the hospital staff so I give them more leeway than I probably should.

In their various school uniforms, darting from seat to seat, they remind me of the restless flocks of parrots that roost in the trees behind my house.

This time, when I got on the train, there were only two other passengers, one at either end.

My intention was to slide the enormous envelope of life-size scans down the side of my seat where it wouldn't get in my way (embarrassingly large print sticker of personal information towards the wall). I'd hold it in place with my foot, then close my eyes and rock on to some vintage rhythm and blues while I recovered my humanity.

While I was trying to jam the envelope in place, I managed to get it tangled in my earphone wires and almost garrotted myself.

"Fuck's sake," I exploded.

Quietly.

In case anyone heard.

I laid the envelope across the seats opposite me, and resting my head on the filthy window, peered down the side of my seat.

There was something wedged in there, so I pulled a pen out of my bag and poked at it until it fell loose.

It was a book.

I looked around the carriage, though I already knew it was as good as empty and no one was going to rush over demanding I leave their book alone.

Grunting a little old lady grunt, I folded myself in half and picked it up off the floor.

Then wiped off the germs on the seat next to my envelope.

It looked like a nicely laminated hardback version of a lurid romance - all bright blue sky, blond woman with heaving bosoms clenched to the bare muscular chest of Mr Tall, Dark and Handsome.

But when I opened it, I found it was a handwritten journal.

With no name or return address on the first page, despite the printed a box suggesting you should write them there.

Maybe it was one of those notebooks where people write a page or two then abandon it for some stranger to add their own touch.

I checked the back pages; no forwarding address, only an expandable pocket containing a fifty dollar note, a myki, and few store receipts.

I checked the carriage again. I'm not sure why, but my sixth sense was tingling.

I was tempted to wedge the book back down beside the seat, pretend I hadn't seen it, and move to another seat somewhere else.

But it was someone's personal book, with cash and transport value.

So, I flicked through the edges of the pages to see if anything leapt out at me.

It was a chaotic jumble of words and pictures in different colours and forms. There were single words, lists and full paragraphs in pencil and pen, highlighted, underlined or starred. Big letters and small, printed, cursive and fancy calligraphy. The images were stickers, drawings and clippings from magazines and newspapers taped onto the pages.

Its randomness reminded me of a Da Vinci notebook.

I couldn't help myself; I checked the carriage yet again.

Still just the three of us, but we'd completed the express section of the journey and were pulling into the first station. Even if the other passengers didn't get off, it was likely the aforementioned school children would be getting on.

I shoved the book in my bag, slid the scans down the side of the seat, and propped the bag between me and the scans. I closed my eyes and leaned against the window, trying to look like that sweet grandma people assume I am.

I'm not exactly sure why.

The sexy cover wasn't the kind of book I normally read. But I wasn't really thinking about the cover, more the content, though I didn't know what it was exactly.

I was nervous about being caught with the book.

It's not that I was embarrassed about having someone else's personal stream of consciousness, more that I'd discovered a delicious secret and didn't want to share it.

Which was hypocritical; I'd be outraged if some stranger kept my journal.

Even though I'd hidden it in my bag, I could feel it burning my hip through the leather, and I couldn't stop thinking about it.

The rest of my journey passed as uneventfully as usual.

Got off the train at my usual unstaffed station, thought about getting a cab, but decided to wait for the bus.

Wrestled the envelope of scans as I trudged up the hill to my house.

Thought once again, I really ought to get an enormous tote bag to carry the bloody things in.

Oscar, my cat, barely opened an eye to acknowledge my homecoming.

While I really wanted to dive straight into the book, the smell of hospital lingered on my skin along with a fine layer of still tacky ultrasound gel.

I took a quick shower and washed my hair before throwing on some old track pants with worn out elastic and a voluminous, stained t-shirt.

Lord knows why I still bother to dress up to go to hospital, it's a waste of a good outfit.

Barefoot, hair still dripping, I walked down to the kitchen. Despite not having eaten all day, I wasn't hungry, so I made some toast with pate and poured a glass of Shiraz.

Not the healthiest snack, but I deserved a treat after the day I'd had.

Oscar strolled in miaowing, rubbing himself against my legs, so I emptied a can of cat tuna in his bowl.

And then it was time.

I sat at my dining table, book in front of me, toast to the left, wine to the right, and a napkin on my lap.

Even when you live alone, and you're dressed like a homeless person, there's no reason to let the civilities slide.

I opened the cover.

I hadn't noticed it on the train, but the pages were lightly scented with a fresh floral fragrance.

Something young and hopeful. The name of it was on the tip of my tongue, but I couldn't bring it to mind. Something with a French name. Something far more sophisticated than the cover of the book would suggest.

Was it something I wore in the long ago?

I sipped my wine, but it didn't help - it was going to annoy me for hours until I came up with the name.

I took a bite of toast and flipped through the first few pages.

A list of contents, an annual calendar glued to the first page, public holidays highlighted in yellow. Two pages of to-dos in business and personal categories. A page of healthy habits to adopt, including exercising, drinking water and meditating.

QUIT SMOKING was in the centre of a box made up of many layers of different colours going around and around the words.

Then another two pages as a monthly calendar with dates and appointments on the left, and to-dos and deadlines on the right. Next, a similar spread for a week, with a daily tracker of weight, steps taken, glasses of water, cigarettes smoked.

How cute.

I wondered if it was helping.

Then days to a page with three bullet-point lists of affirmations and to-dos at the top, and paragraphs about the day's achievements and things to remember for tomorrow.

The daily pages were interspersed with things like meeting notes, voice mail transcriptions, and book quotes.

As well as longer passages where the owner worked through issues that bothered her.

I say her because it didn't seem likely a bloke was going to write a list reminding himself to eat yoghurt, use a body brush or wash his face before bed.

And it seemed the girl was a bit neurotic.

Perhaps that's too harsh an assessment; she was probably just young enough, say early twenties, to still think she could control everything.

Or, it could be that post-cancer, I'm just bitter and scornful.

Plus, it was quite like my own journalling system.

Several hours later, I finished reading as the sun was setting in a wash of red and purple.

I felt unsettled and disturbed. Maybe a bit sucked in.

I emptied the glass in almost one swallow and poured myself another.

Oscar leapt into my lap, and I scratched his chin as I reviewed what I had read.

The writer was some kind of freelancer working from home.

Some days she was happy with her progress and gave herself a cheerful kawaii sticker as a reward.

Other times she was less happy and rebuked herself for getting side-tracked and ignoring her most important work.

And in between the story of her attempts to grow a thriving business, was a more personal story of her search for love.

She'd met a boy who made her heart sing.

He was caring, an incredible lover, and loved to cook.

One day he stayed over and never left. She was ecstatic.

Not much later, he got jealous and controlling.

He started criticising her intelligence and appearance.

She started to doubt herself, and her business suffered.

She wondered how to make him move out of what had become more his home than hers.

Then, for reasons she didn't understand, he started hitting her and threatened to kill her.

And then the book had ended, about 50 pages from the end.

"He's going to kill me. I've got to get out of here." were the last words.

Now, white hair notwithstanding, I am not old, married, or sweet.

What I am is independent, cynical and like to keep myself to myself.

I stood up, dumping Oscar, and took my wine out onto the deck. I stood looking out over the immaculate garden I pay someone else to take care of.

I turned my face to the last of the sun, closed my eyes and listened to the avian version of Twilight Barking.

The way I saw it, the book was either fact or fiction. Either some kind of immersive role-playing game or the record of a young woman's descent into hell.

If it was true, and there was a girl out there in grave danger, then something had to be done.

And if it wasn't, I risked looking like a fool.

We all like to think we'd do the "right thing," and some of us probably would.

But no one wants to stand outside the common herd, and we're not going to risk our place by drawing attention to ourselves.

We all place more emphasis on our imagined reputations as credible and responsible people than we really ought.

So, there were several elements that suggested a factual basis:

- The book was a chaotic assembly of random notes and thoughts, some clear and legible, some scrawled and indecipherable without careful study.
- There was cash and a myki.

- In a planned and composed nook, the writing would've been neater and more consistent throughout.
- While somewhat melodramatic, the "story" was plausible, and sadly, quite common.
- The "story" ended in the middle of itself, and with plenty of pages left in the book.

But on the other hand

- There was a recent, well-publicised terrorism case where a man had stolen a colleague's notebook and computer codes, researched and written some incriminating notes, then handed the results into the Federal Police to implicate his colleague, clearing his way to make a move on the girlfriend.
- If you were in trouble, would you *really* rely on some stranger for help and not go to your close friends and family?
- It was conceivable that leaving the book on the train was a way of symbolically letting go of that life before escaping into a new one.

I was deeply suspicious of the truth of the journal, but I wasn't confident enough in my doubt to do nothing.

No matter which way I looked at it, I found myself morally lacking, and that disturbed me.

I *wanted* to think of myself as the kind of person who helps strangers regardless.

And I wanted to believe that were I in need, someone would come to my aid.

But if I wouldn't take up someone else's cause, how could I expect anyone to take up mine?

If nothing else, the book, the cash and myki were lost property.

Whether lost or planted, someone had to do something.

I'm not Miss Marple, so the least I could do was hand the problem over to better minds than mine to decide what, if anything, was required.

By this stage, I was not just exhausted, but bone-weary, dog-tired and done for too.

The only thing left to do was to sleep on it. Maybe the answer would be clearer in the morning.

Oscar followed me to bed, but we both spent a restless night, and the Summer heat wasn't the only cause.

The next day, I showered and dressed like a respectable, community-minded citizen, and walked down to the train station.

I travelled a couple of stops, not looking down the side of the seat, then walked to my closest police station.

It was empty, so I rang the bell for attention.

In a short while, a young officer came through and asked, "Can I help you Ma'am?"

I still wasn't sure how I felt about the book, so I started with the lost property angle.

"I found this book on the train yesterday," I said, placing it on the counter and nudging it under the security wires.

"It looks like a personal journal, but there's cash and a myki in the back."

"Thank you," she said, handing over a pen and a form "please fill this out. If no one claims it within three months, you get to keep it, and we'll be in touch to arrange collection."

"Um, OK, thanks.

"Thing is," I said, face flushing, "I read it to see if I could find out who owns it, and while I don't know if it's real, I'm concerned about the woman who wrote it."

"I see."

"She writes about the deterioration of her relationship and abuse at the hands of her boyfriend, and if true, she might be in danger."

"I see."

The officer picked up the book and flicked through it as I filled in the form, sneaking looks at her face as I did.

It remained impassive, and I wondered a little hysterically if police officers take classes to train their outward reactions.

As I laid the pen down, she snapped the book shut, face still impressively expressionless, and laid it aside.

She read through my form, filled in the receipt section, tore it off and handed it to me.

"Very well Ms Jones, I'll pass this through to the detectives for further investigation. Thank you for your concern."

And then she turned smartly and disappeared with the book and my form out back.

I leapt out the police station door and stood panting by the side of the road for a moment.

Thank God that was over.

I didn't know whether they'd investigate or not. And I didn't know if I'd ever find out what happened or not.

But I knew I'd done the right thing.

I could rest comfortably knowing I'd done what little I could to preserve the young woman's life. I don't know if that will help restore her faith in humanity, but it restored my faith in me.

THE END

ABOUT THE AUTHOR

Alexandria Blaelock writes stories, some of them for *Ellery Queen's Mystery Magazine* and *Pulphouse Fiction Magazine*. She's also written four self-help books applying business techniques to personal matters like getting dressed, cleaning house, and feeding your friends.

As a recovering Project Manager, she's probably too fond of sticking to plan. She lives in a forest because she enjoys birdsong, the scent of gum leaves and the sun on her face. When not telecommuting to parallel universes from her Melbourne based imagination, she watches K-dramas, talks to animals, and drinks Campari. At the same time.

Discover more at www.alexandriablaelock.com.

OTHER SHORT STORIES BY ALEXANDRIA BLAELOCK

Kiss of Death
Long Weekend in the Snow
Shining Star
Phoenix Child
Ship in a Bottle
Lady of the Looking Glass
Simone Says Hands in the Air
Life in the Security Directorate
Fate in Your Hands
Love in the Security Directorate
Alma's Grace
Payton's Run
The Guardian's Vigil
The Life and Death of Carmelita Basingstoke
Balancing the Book

BOOKS BY ALEXANDRIA BLAELOCK

Stress Free Dinner Parties
Build Your Signature Wardrobe
Holistic Personal Finance
Ms Blaelock's Book of Minimally Viable
Housekeeping

Ingram Content Group UK Ltd.
Milton Keynes UK
UKHW020715210423
420559UK00016B/1079

9 781925 749304